SCOOBY-DOO!
An Early Reading Adventure
THE MISSING SCOOBY-SNACKS

By Robin Wasserman
Illustrated by Duendes del Sur

ABDOPUBLISHING.COM

Reinforced library bound edition published in 2017 by Spotlight, a division of ABDO. PO Box 398166, Minneapolis, Minnesota 55439. Spotlight produces high-quality reinforced library bound editions for schools and libraries. Published by agreement with Warner Bros. Entertainment Inc.

Printed in the United States of America, North Mankato, Minnesota.
042016   092016

THIS BOOK CONTAINS
RECYCLED MATERIALS

PUBLISHER'S CATALOGING IN PUBLICATION DATA

Names: Wasserman, Robin, author. I Duendes del Sur, illustrator.
Title: Scooby-Doo and the missing Scooby-snacks / by Robin Wasserman ; illustrated by Duendes del Sur.
Description: Minneapolis, MN : Spotlight, [2017] I Series: Scooby-Doo early reading adventures
Summary: Scooby and the gang are on a camping trip. But someone's been sneaking around their campsite and now their Scooby-Snacks are gone! Did a monster take the Scooby-Snacks? It's up to Scooby to sniff out the culprit!
Identifiers: LCCN 2016930648 I ISBN 9781614794677 (lib. bdg.)
Subjects: LCSH: Scooby-Doo (Fictitious character)--Juvenile fiction. I Dogs--Juvenile fiction. I Camping--Juvenile fiction. I Monsters--Juvenile fiction. I Mystery and detective stories--Juvenile fiction. I Adventure and adventurers--Juvenile fiction.
Classification: DDC [Fic]--dc23
LC record available at http://lccn.loc.gov/2016930648

Spotlight
A Division of ABDO
abdopublishing.com

Scooby and the gang were on a camping trip.

It was a beautiful day for a swim in the lake.

The sun was shining and not a cloud was in the sky.

"Like, this is fun, but I'm hungry!" Shaggy said.

When Scooby, Shaggy and Fred
returned to the campsite, it was
not how they had left it.
All of their belongings were on
the ground.
"Like, someone's been eating
our food," said Shaggy.
"Someone's been wearing my
shirt," said Fred.
"Ruh-oh," said Scooby.
The Scooby-Snacks were
missing!

Velma picked up Daphne's torn shirt.

"I don't understand what happened," she said.

"Only a monster could have destroyed my favorite shirt!" said Daphne.

"Monster!" said Shaggy. He jumped into the Mystery Machine to hide. Scooby buried himself under a pile of leaves.

"We need to find our Scooby-Snacks," said Shaggy.

"Let's search for clues," said Fred.

The gang went to look for clues
around the lake.
They found their flashlight and
a soda can on a dirt path.
"I think we are on the right
track," Velma said.
"Scooby, do you smell any
Scooby-Snacks?" Fred asked.
Scooby shook his head.
Just then, Daphne noticed
something.
"Look!" she cried.

Daphne found giant paw prints.

"Ronster!" yelped Scooby.

"Look!" said Velma.

Velma found her book on the ground.

It had large scratches across the cover.

"Jinkies!" Velma said. "I have a hunch about who might have taken our Scooby-Snacks, and we're going to need some help."

Fred, Daphne and Velma went
to look for a park ranger.
Scooby and Shaggy sat down on
a rock to wait.
All the waiting was making
them hungry.
"Like, I wish I had some
Scooby-Snacks," said Shaggy.
"Re too!" said Scooby.
"Let's go find them!" Shaggy
said.
"Rokay," said Scooby.

Scooby used his super sense of smell to search for the Scooby-Snacks.

It led through the forest to a cave.

Scooby and Shaggy looked inside.

It was very dark in the cave.

Scooby could not see anything, but he smelled Scooby-Snacks.

Scooby was scared, but he wanted to find the Scooby-Snacks.

"Do you smell Scooby-Snacks?" Shaggy asked him.

Scooby nodded.

"Like, follow your nose, Scoob!" said Shaggy.

They couldn't believe what they found.

All their missing food was piled high, and the Scooby-Snacks were on top!

Just then, Scooby and Shaggy
heard a noise.

Roooooaaar!

"Like, I think it's the monster,"
Shaggy said.

"Oh no! I was wrong. It's a bear!
Run!" yelled Shaggy.

Shaggy ran out of the cave.

But the bear grabbed hold of
Scooby's tail.

Then, something unexpected
happened.

The bear smiled at Scooby and
gave him a hug.

Scooby wasn't so comfortable
with this.

But the bear offered to share the
Scooby-Snacks.

Soon, Scooby and the bear were eating Scooby-Snacks together! Scooby had made a new friend and solved the mystery.

Fred, Daphne and Velma returned with a ranger to help.

"Looks like there isn't a monster after all," said Daphne.

The End